There's a Billy Goat in the Garden

Based on a Puerto Rican folk tale

retold by Laurel Dee Gugler

illustrated by Clare Beaton

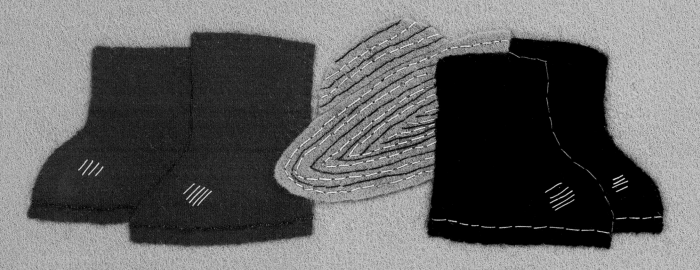

Barefoot Books
Celebrating Art and Story

There's a billy goat in the garden
and he will NOT come out.

"I'll chase that goat," says the rooster.
He flutters all about.
But that huffy, gruff old billy goat
will NOT COME OUT!

There's a billy goat in the garden
and he will NOT come out.
"I'm bigger," barks the dog.

He yip-yaps all about.
But that haughty, naughty billy goat
will NOT COME OUT!

There's a billy goat in the garden
and he will NOT come out.
"I'm bigger," grunts the pig.

He sniff-snorts all about.
But that fighting, biting billy goat
will NOT COME OUT!

There's a billy goat in the garden
and he will NOT come out.
"I'm bigger," brays the donkey.

He clip-clops all about.
But that dancing, prancing billy goat
will NOT COME OUT!

There's a billy goat in the garden
and he will NOT come out.
"I'm bigger," moos the cow.

She bustles all about.
But that surly, burly billy goat
will NOT come out!

There's a billy goat in the garden
and he will NOT come out.
"I'm bigger," neighs the horse.

He gallops all about.
But that stomping, tromping billy goat
will NOT come out!

There's a billy goat in the garden
and he will NOT come out.
"Watch me," says tiny bee.
He buzzes all about.

"But you're tiny," laugh the animals.
They snicker, snort and shout.
"You silly, itty-bitty bee
YOU CAN'T CHASE THAT GOAT OUT!"

CRASH

Z-Z-ZIP-ZOOM-VROOM!
Bee buzzes all about.
and that smashing, crashing billy goat
DOES COME OUT!

Praise for Clare Beaton

How Loud is a Lion?
"The fine craft-work of beads, embroidery, and appliqué, and the great endpapers with
an assortment of slithering snakes are stunning" — *School Library Journal*

How Big is a Pig?
"Bold, bright tableaux...a sassy, unexpected wrap-up; Beaton will have her audience's
attention all sewn up" — *Publishers Weekly*

Mother Goose Remembers
"She exquisitely and inventively crafts each picture" — *Publishers Weekly*

Zoë and her Zebra
"A useful teaching tool which is highly attractive"
— *Early Years Educator*

**For Carol and the girls and boys at Hesston Community Child Care — L. D. G.
For Cath — C. B.**

Barefoot Books
2067 Massachusetts Avenue
Cambridge MA 02140

This book was typeset in 20 on 28 point Plantin Schoolbook Bold
The illustrations were prepared in felt with braid, beads and sequins
Graphic design by Judy Linard, London.
Color transparencies by Jonathan Fisher Photography, Bath
Color separation by Grafiscan, Italy.
Printed and bound in Singapore by Tien Wah Press Pte Ltd
This book has been printed on 100% acid-free paper

Library of Congress Cataloging-in-Publication Data
Gugler, Laurel Dee.
    There's a billy goat in the garden / Laurel Dee Gugler ; Clare Beaton. 1st ed.
[24] p. : col. ill. ;   cm.
Summary: A rowdy group of farmyard animals flutter, snort, stomp and tromp,
trying to chase a stubborn, old billy goat out of the garden. But it is the most
unlikely animal _ a tiny bee _ who actually manages to do it.
ISBN 1-84148-089-4
1. Animals _ Fiction. 2. Goats _ Fiction. I. Beaton, Clare. II. Title.
  [E] 21 2003

3 5 7 9 8 6 4

Barefoot Books
Celebrating Art and Story

At Barefoot Books, we celebrate art and story
with books that open the hearts and minds of children
from all walks of life, inspiring them to read deeper,
search further, and explore their own creative gifts.
Taking our inspiration from many different cultures,
we focus on themes that encourage independence of
spirit, enthusiasm for learning, and acceptance of
other traditions. Thoughtfully prepared by writers,
artists and storytellers from all over the world, our
products combine the best of the present with the
best of the past to educate our children as the
caretakers of tomorrow.

www.barefootbooks.com